MINETTE'S FEAST

The Delicious Story of Julia Child and Her Cat

By
Susanna Reich

Illustrated by
Amy Bates

Abrams Books for Young Readers, New York

In memory of my grandmother, Anita Reich,
who showed me how to love cats, and to Tigger,
Don Quixote, Bubelah, Fluffy, and Chloe
—S.R.

For Alex, the coolest cat I know
—A.B.

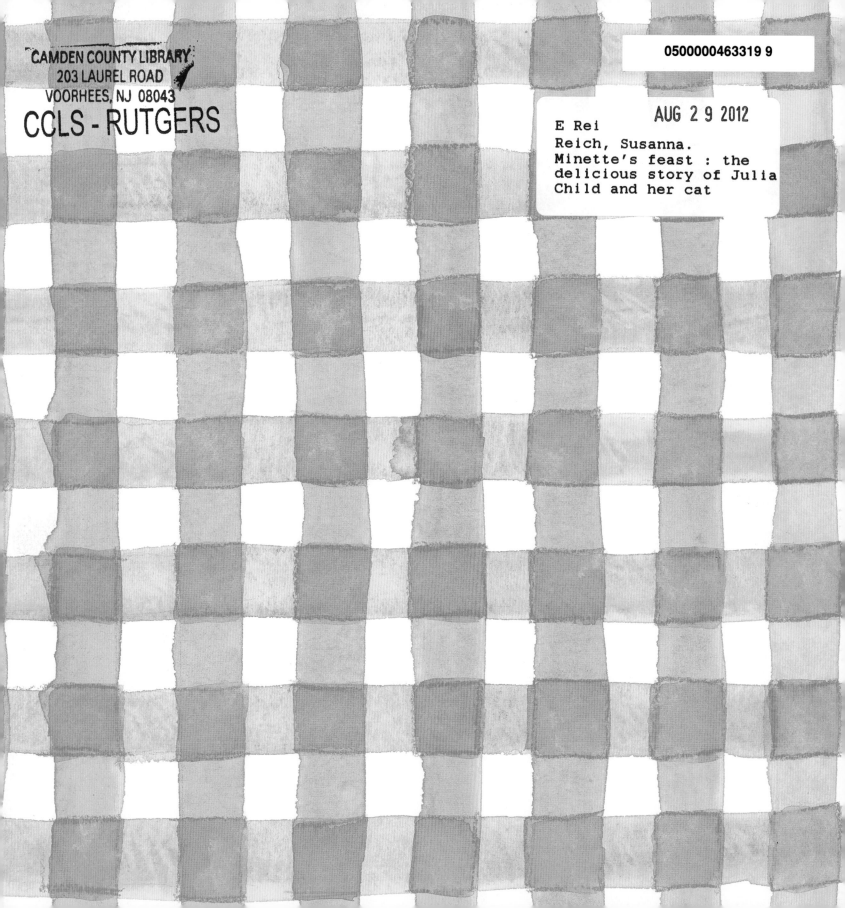

The illustrations in this book
were created using pencil and watercolor.

Library of Congress Cataloging-in-Publication Data

Reich, Susanna.
Minette's Feast : the delicious story of Julia Child and her cat / by Susanna Reich ; illustrated by Amy Bates.
p. cm.
Includes bibliographical references.
Summary: While Julia is in the kitchen learning to cook up elaborate, delicious dishes, the only feast Minette is
truly interested in is that of fresh mouse. Includes biographical information about Julia Child.
ISBN 978-1-4197-0177-1
[1. Child, Julia—Fiction. 2. Cats—Fiction. 3. Cooking, French—Fiction. 4. Food habits—Fiction. 5. Paris
(France)—Fiction. 6. France—Fiction.] I. Bates, Amy June, ill. II. Title.
PZ7.R26343Mi 2012
[E]—dc23
2011034275

Book design by Chad W. Beckerman

Photo of Julia Child and Minette, Paris, ca. 1950, by Paul Child courtesy of the Schlesinger Library,
Radcliffe Institute, Harvard University.

Printed and bound in China
10 9 8 7 6 5 4 3 2

Abrams Books for Young Readers are available at special discounts when purchased in quantity for
premiums and promotions as well as fundraising or educational use. Special editions can also be created to
specification. For details, contact specialsales@abramsbooks.com or the address below.

ABRAMS
THE ART OF BOOKS SINCE 1949
115 West 18th Street
New York, NY 10011
www.abramsbooks.com

MINETTE Mimosa McWilliams Child was a very lucky cat, perhaps the luckiest cat in all of Paris.

Day and night she could hear the bells of Sainte-Clotilde tolling the hour.

And day and night she could smell the delicious smells of mayonnaise, hollandaise, cassoulets, cheese soufflés, and duck pâtés wafting from the pots and pans of her owner, Julia Child.

But life had not always been like this for Minette.

Oh no, not at all.

Several years earlier, Julia Child had moved to Paris with her husband, Paul.

They had no children, nor did they have any pets.

But they had each other.

Every weekend, arm-in-arm, they wandered down the cobblestone streets, poking into little shops and peeking into hidden courtyards.

And every time they went out for a walk, they enjoyed a fine, fine meal.

They nibbled croissants in cafés where cats curled on chairs.

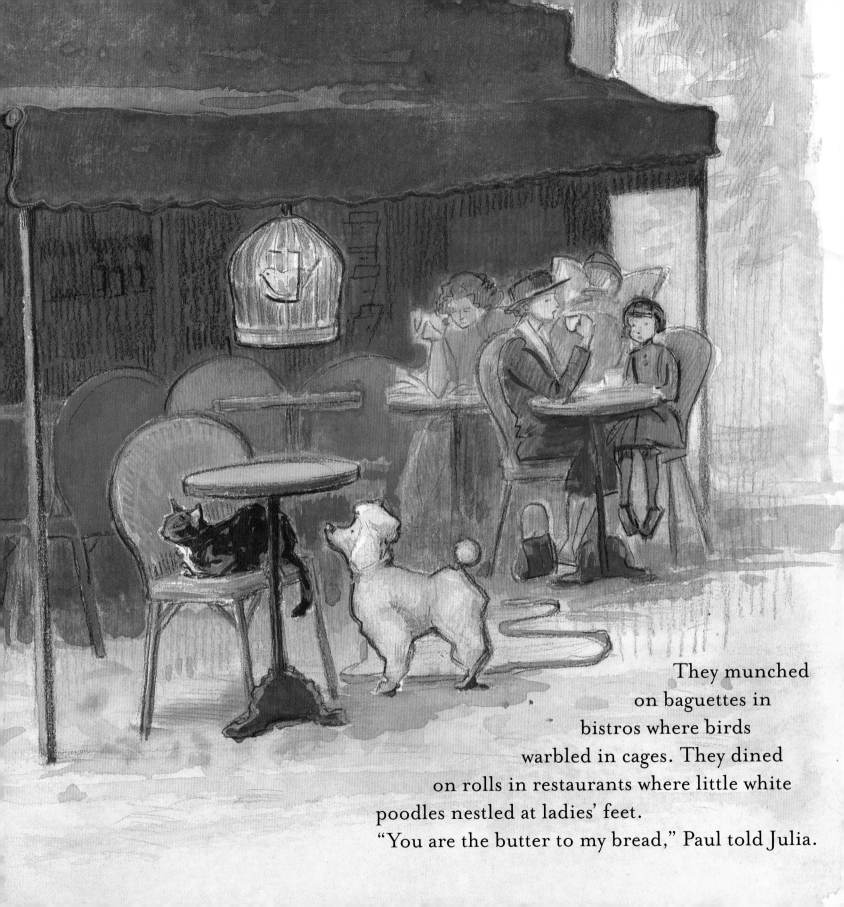

They munched
on baguettes in
bistros where birds
warbled in cages. They dined
on rolls in restaurants where little white
poodles nestled at ladies' feet.
"You are the butter to my bread," Paul told Julia.

Julia and Paul's apartment was dark—and so cold in the winter that they had to wear coats in the living room.

There were birds on the windowsill—and mice in the walls.

The kitchen was up a narrow flight of stairs, and there was no refrigerator, only an icebox.

But this was home, and Julia and Paul warmed it with family and friends.

There was only one thing missing.

"*Une maison sans chat, c'est la vie sans soleil!*"
"A house without a cat is like life without sunshine!"
And so Julia and Paul adopted Minette, a mischievous,
energetic *poussiequette* with a lovely speckled coat.
Or, shall we say, Minette adopted Julia and Paul.

Julia and Paul were charmed by Minette's delicate
whiskers, her superior nose, and her quick little paws.

Here was a cat who thoroughly enjoyed life's many pleasures—long naps, soft laps, and, of course, lunch. But for Minette, no ordinary meal would do.

Like any self-respecting French cat, Minette wouldn't dream of eating food out of a can.

What a thrill to pounce on an unsuspecting bird!

How delightful the crunch of fresh-caught mouse, devoured on the living room rug!

Julia spent mornings at the marketplace, buying meat from *le boucher*, bread from *le boulanger*, milk and cheese from *la crémière*, and cake from *le pâtissier*.

Afterward, she'd make a splendid lunch for herself and Paul, and offer Minette the leftovers.

Minette might even take a nibble.

But of course, mouse and bird were much preferred.

Sometimes, the "nice old fish lady" at the marketplace gave Julia luscious fish heads for Minette.

Julia would cook them up in a pot.

Perhaps she'd add a dollop of scrumptious "chicken liver custard."

Minette might even take a nibble.

But it seemed that mouse and bird were really much preferred.

Julia was determined to improve her cooking, so she went to the marketplace for advice.

At the vegetable stand, an old lady showed her "how to tell a good potato from a bad one."

At the supply store, Julia bought "enough knives to fill a pirate ship."

She carted home a giant cookbook, and she even learned how to stir "two pots at the same time."

Minette was not impressed.

And so Julia signed up for classes at Le Cordon
Bleu, the famous cooking school.

When Chef Bugnard, the teacher, taught her to slice
and dice, mince and chop, she paid close attention.

"I had never taken anything so seriously," she later
wrote. "Husband and cat excepted."

At home, Minette took her job seriously, too.

She perfected her hunting skills by chasing "a
Brussels sprout tied to a string."

As the months passed, Julia became quite the gourmet cook.

She baked and blanched, blended and boiled, drained and dried, dusted and fried.

She floured and flipped, pitted and plucked, rinsed and roasted, sizzled and skimmed.

And when she wasn't trimming, toasting, or topping, she was washing, whipping, and whisking!

At Julia's feet, Minette purred with contentment.
The smells were heavenly, the tastes delightful.

Still, there was mouse.

One chilly fall morning, Julia
decided to test a new recipe.
Perhaps it would be even
better than mouse.

She went to the marketplace and bought a special cut of meat.

She rubbed it with salt and pepper and showered it with herbs and spices.

Then she placed it on the windowsill and waited for the flavors to develop.

For three days.

Minette waited, too.

Finally, the meat was ready to cook.

Julia eased it into a pan, tucked some
vegetables around it, and popped the pan
in the oven.

The meat bubbled and spat.

When it was done, Julia proudly carried
the platter to the table.

Ooh-la-la!
Magnifique!

For three days, Julia and Paul feasted on the leftovers while Minette waited for a nibble. When Julia finally laid the platter on the floor, bits of meat still clung to the bone. "Would you like to try this, *poussiequette*?" said Julia.

Minette crept up to the platter.

She sniffed.
She twitched.

And then she pounced.
Ooh-la-la!
Magnifique!

Minette attacked that bone, gnawing it and chewing it and rolling it around on the floor.

She frisked and flounced, darted and batted. She tiptoed and hopped, danced and pranced.

She jumped and rolled, curled and stretched, raced and ran, gurgled and purred.

And then she licked herself all over and took a nice long nap.

Minette Mimosa McWilliams Child was a very lucky cat, perhaps the luckiest cat in all of Paris.

She lived upstairs in an old gray house, one block from the River Seine.

Day and night she could hear the bells of Sainte-Clotilde tolling the hour.

And day and night she could smell the delicious smells of mayonnaise, hollandaise, cassoulets, cheese soufflés, and duck pâtés wafting from the pots and pans of her owner, Julia Child.

Bon appétit, Minette!

Still . . .
There would always be mouse.

AFTERWORD

Julia McWilliams Child (August 15, 1912–August 13, 2004) revolutionized the way Americans eat. Her career was launched in 1961 with the publication of *Mastering the Art of French Cooking*, coauthored with two French friends, Simone "Simca" Beck and Louisette Bertholle. After the debut of Julia's award-winning public television show *The French Chef* in 1963, she became the most famous cook in America. Despite the name of the show, she never referred to herself as a chef, because she had never cooked professionally in a restaurant.

Born to a prosperous family in Pasadena, California, Julia McWilliams was known in school for her outgoing personality, creative spirit, and athletic skills. She stood out in another way, too. By the time she enrolled at Smith, an elite women's college in Northampton, Massachusetts, Julia was six feet two inches tall. She graduated in 1934 with a bachelor's degree in English and no cooking skills whatsoever.

Julia Child and Minette, Paris, ca. 1950. Photo by Paul Child.

At the time, few women of Julia's social class worked outside the home. But with no marriage prospects on the horizon, Julia needed something to do. She worked for two years as an advertising copywriter in New York City. When her mother passed away, she returned to Pasadena to live with her father. There she hosted parties, wrote plays and book reviews, and volunteered for charity.

When World War II broke out, Julia wanted to contribute to the war effort. Too tall to join the Women's Army Corps or the Navy's WAVES, she moved to Washington, D.C., and found work with the Office of Strategic Services, the precursor to the CIA. In 1944, she was sent to Ceylon (now Sri Lanka), where she met fellow employee Paul Child, a sophisticated artist and writer who was ten years older than Julia—and quite a bit shorter. Later, they were both posted to China, where their mutual interest in Chinese cuisine drew them closer together. When not eating, Julia handled secret communications.

After the war, Julia and Paul returned to the United States, and in 1946 they were married. She settled into the role of wife and Washington hostess while Paul pursued a career with the U.S. Foreign Service. In 1948, Paul was posted to Paris as an exhibits officer with the U.S. Information Agency. There the couple adopted Minette, a tricolored tortoiseshell, the first of their many cats. Minette acquired the middle name Mimosa after nibbling the flowers off a mimosa branch that Julia had brought home.

In 1949, Julia started classes at L'École du Cordon Bleu. Three years later, she opened a cooking school in her Paris apartment with Simca and Louisette. It was a late start for a career, but Julia made up for it.

"The more I cook, the more I like to cook," she wrote at the time. "To think that it has taken me forty years to find my true creative hobby and passion (cat and husband excepted)."

By the time *Mastering the Art of French Cooking* was published, the Foreign Service had posted the Childs not just to Paris but also to Marseilles, France; Plittersdorf, Germany; and Oslo, Norway.

Julia's career took off just as Paul's was winding down, and when he retired they settled in Cambridge, Massachusetts. Julia went on to create many more cookbooks and numerous television series, and to found the American Institute of Wine and Food with several fellow gastronomes. Even when she was in her eighties, she barely slowed down.

"*Boutez en avant!*" she would shout. "Full steam ahead!"

Julia once described a friend as a "swallow-life-in-big-gulps" kind of person. The same could be said of her.

She died in Montecito, California, in 2004, two days before her ninety-second birthday.

It is not known when Minette died, although it can be said with some certainty that she died a well-fed cat.

NOTES

None of the dialogue in this book is invented. It is found in *My Life in France* and in Julia and Paul's letters, which are quoted in that book as well as in Noël Riley Fitch's *Appetite for Life*. The original letters are in the collection of the Arthur and Elizabeth Schlesinger Library on the History of Women in America, Radcliffe Institute, Harvard University.

"You are the butter to my bread": Paul Child letter to Charles Child, spring 1951, quoted in Fitch, *Appetite for Life,* p. 183.

"*Une maison sans chat*": Child, *My Life in France*, p. 266.

"nice old fish lady": Ibid., p. 54.

"chicken liver custard": see the recipe for *Timbales de Foies de Volaille* [Unmolded Chicken Liver Custards] in Child, *Mastering the Art of French Cooking*, p. 174.

"how to tell a good potato": Child, *My Life in France*, p. 40.

"enough knives to fill a pirate ship": Ibid., p. 73.

"two pots at the same time": Paul Child letter to Charles Child, mid-December 1949, quoted in Child, *My Life in France*, p. 72.

"I had never taken anything so seriously": Child, *My Life in France*, p. 63.

"a Brussels sprout tied to a string": Ibid., p. 36.

"Would you like to try this": Ibid., p. 113.

"The more I cook": Julia Child letter to Fredericka Child, spring 1952, quoted in Fitch, *Appetite for Life,* p. 191.

"*Boutez en avant!*": Fitch, *Appetite for Life,* p. 436.

"swallow-life-in-big-gulps": Child, *My Life in France*, p. 37.

SOURCES

Child, Julia. "Fall Feasting: France and Spain; In Praise of Partridge." *New York Times*, Oct. 21, 1990.

Child, Julia, Louisette Bertholle, and Simone Beck. *Mastering the Art of French Cooking*. New York: Alfred A. Knopf, 1961.

Child, Julia, and Simone Beck. *Mastering the Art of French Cooking*, vol. 2. New York: Alfred A. Knopf, 1970.

Child, Julia, with Alex Prud'homme. *My Life in France*. New York: Anchor Books, 2006.

Fitch, Noël Riley. *Appetite for Life: The Biography of Julia Child*. New York: Doubleday, 1997.

Shapiro, Laura. *Julia Child: A Life*. New York: Viking, 2007.

The entire kitchen from Julia's Cambridge, Massachusetts, home is now in the collection of the Smithsonian National Museum of American History. An online exhibit can be seen at: http://americanhistory.si.edu/juliachild/

GLOSSARY AND PRONUNCIATION GUIDE

le boucher (luh boo-SHAY) — the butcher

le boulanger (luh boo-lon-ZHAY) — the baker

cassoulet (cah-soo-LAY) — a rich, savory stew containing white beans and a variety of meats

cheese soufflé (soo-FLAY) — a light, fluffy baked dish made with beaten egg whites, egg yolks, white sauce, and cheese

la crémière (la crem-ee-AIR) — the dairywoman

hollandaise (hah-lan-DAYS) — a creamy sauce made with butter, egg yolks, and lemon juice

Magnifique! (mon-yee-FEEK) — Magnificent!

Une maison sans chat, c'est la vie sans soleil! (Oon may-ZON san shah, say la vee san so-LAY) — A house without a cat is like a day without sunshine!

Ooh-la-la! — Oh my!

pâté (pah-TAY) — a spread made of finely ground cooked meat, such as pork, duck, or liver

le pâtissier (luh pah-tee-see-AY) — the pastry maker

poussiequette (poo-see-KET) [not a real French word] — pussycat

AUTHOR'S NOTE

When I was a child, I loved watching *The French Chef*. I was entranced by Julia's energy, sense of humor, and unapologetic enthusiasm for cooking and eating.

I had the honor of meeting her in 1993 when I designed the floral decorations for her eightieth birthday party, a gala affair at the legendary Rainbow Room in New York City. The centerpieces were made of white lilacs, red roses, and white orchids. In the middle of each arrangement stood an eighteen-inch wire whisk with a red rose inside, a token of not only my affection for Julia but the affection of the entire New York food world. I also created Julia's official birthday present for the occasion—a gigantic forty-eight-inch industrial whisk festooned with white orchids and faux pearls. When the gift was presented to her, she grinned and slung it over her shoulder.

Not long after, I began to write children's books. Julia lurked in the back of my mind as someone I would like to write about, but I could never figure out how to make the story interesting to children. Then I read Julia's memoir, *My Life in France*, and discovered Minette, who inspired Julia's lifelong love of cats. As a cat lover myself, I knew I had finally found my story. My cat, Chloe, couldn't have agreed more.

Of course, Minette was not the reason that Julia wanted to become a better cook or why she enrolled in Le Cordon Bleu—she thought of that all on her own. And Julia never actually said that Minette preferred mouse. But anyone who has ever lived with a cat knows that leftovers, no matter how delectable, can never compete with mouse.